Iguanodon

Tyrannosaurus rex

Parasaurolophus

Brachiosaurus

Silvisaurus

Ankylosaurus

Stegosaurus

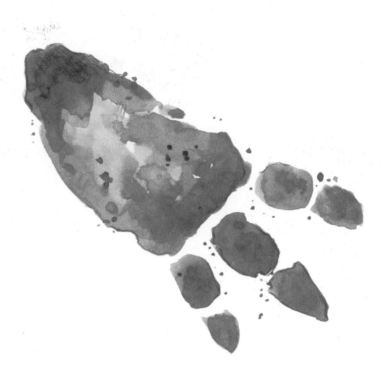
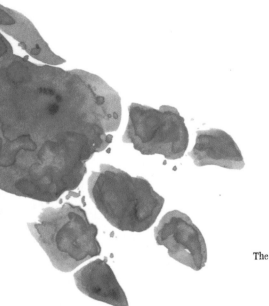

For Mum, Dad and Mark

First published **2016** by Nosy Crow Ltd
The Crow's Nest, **10a** Lant Street
London SE1 1QR
www.nosycrow.com

ISBN 978 0 85763 517 4 (HB)
ISBN 978 0 85763 613 3 (PB)

Nosy Crow and associated logos are trademarks
and/or registered trademarks of Nosy Crow Ltd.

Text and illustrations © Lucy Volpin **2016**

The right of Lucy Volpin to be identified as the author and illustrator of this work has been asserted.

A CIP catalogue record for this book is available from the British Library.

Printed in China by Imago

Papers used by Nosy Crow are made from wood grown in
sustainable forests.

1 3 5 7 9 8 6 4 2 (HB)
1 3 5 7 9 8 6 4 2 (PB)

WE LOVE DINOSAURS

Lucy Volpin

nosy crow

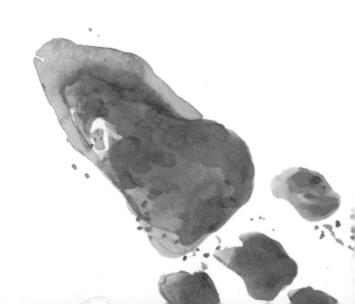

We love
ones that
are really

tall.

We love ones
that are only
small.

We love ones that can **gallop** past...

and **plodding** ones that don't go fast.

We love ones that like
leaves
to eat...

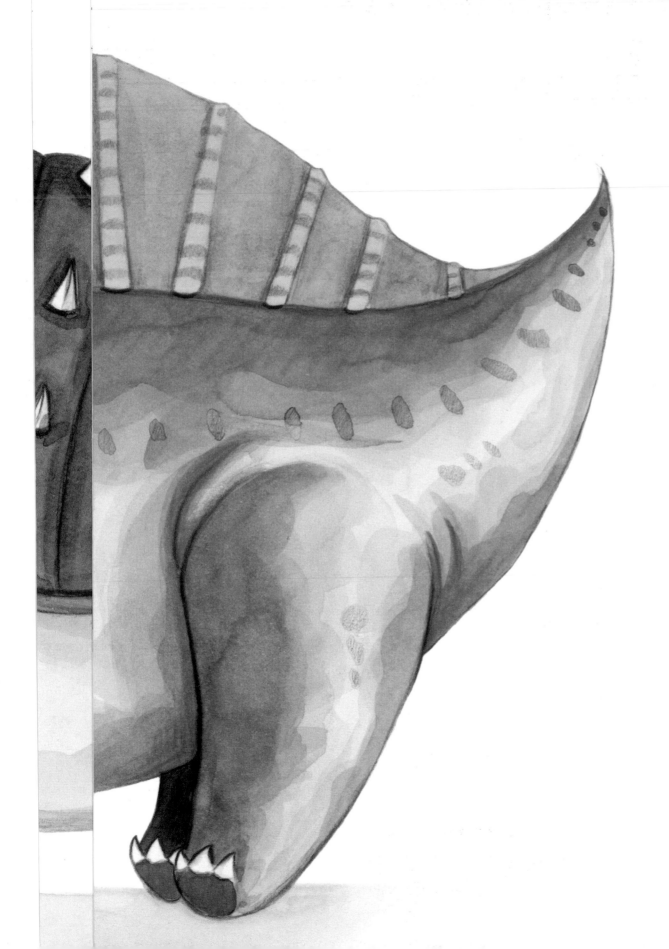

and ones
that like a
meaty
treat.

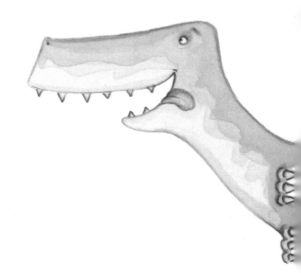

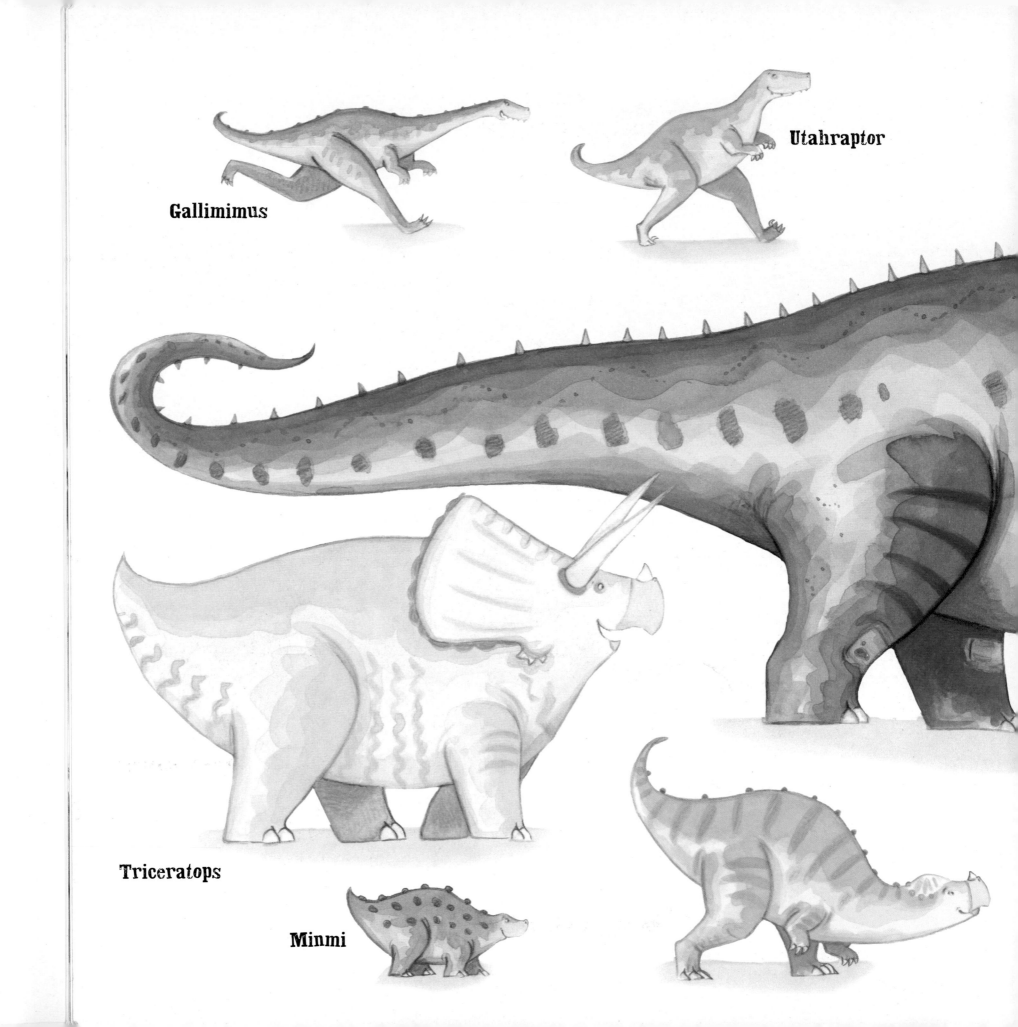

Gallimimus

Utahraptor

Triceratops

Minmi

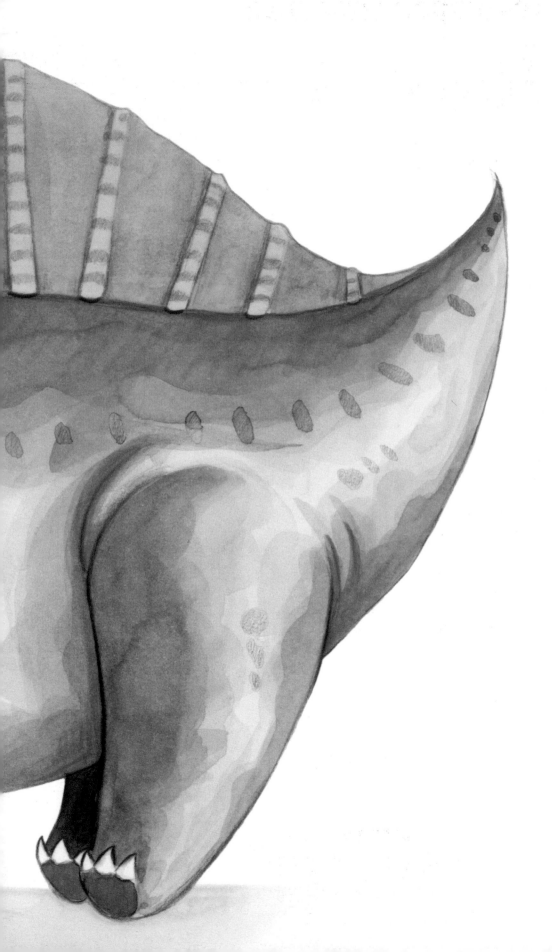

and ones
that like a
meaty
treat.

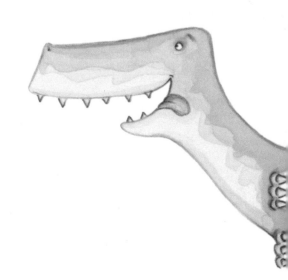

We love ones with **gigantic**...

ROARS!

And ones with tiny, **snuffly** snores.

We love their **spines**
from **head** to **tail.**

We love the **spikes**

they **swing**

and **flail.**

...we **really wish**
they weren't...

We love the **spikes**
they **swing**
and **flail.**

We love their **spots** and **zigzag** tums...

their
scratchy
claws and
pointy
thumbs.

We love the ones that **fight**

and
brawl.

In fact, we **really** love them **all!**

The **more** we **learn**, the **more** we **think**...

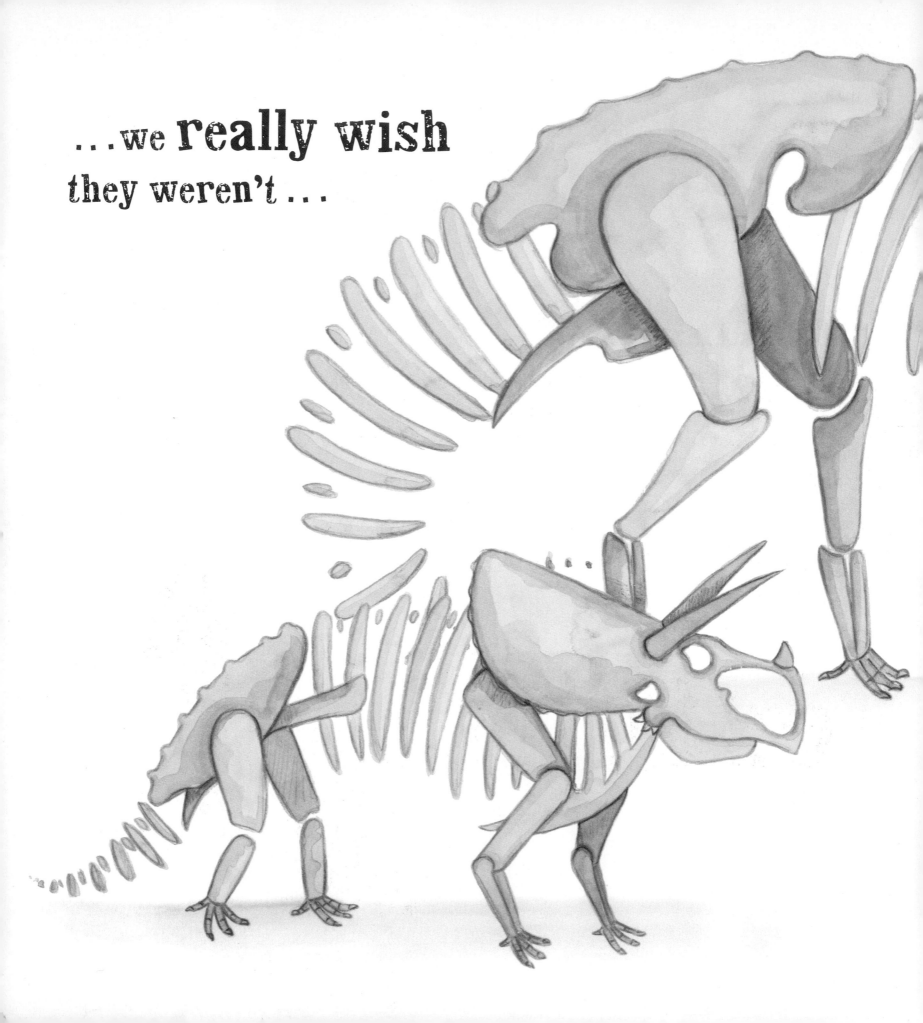

extinct.

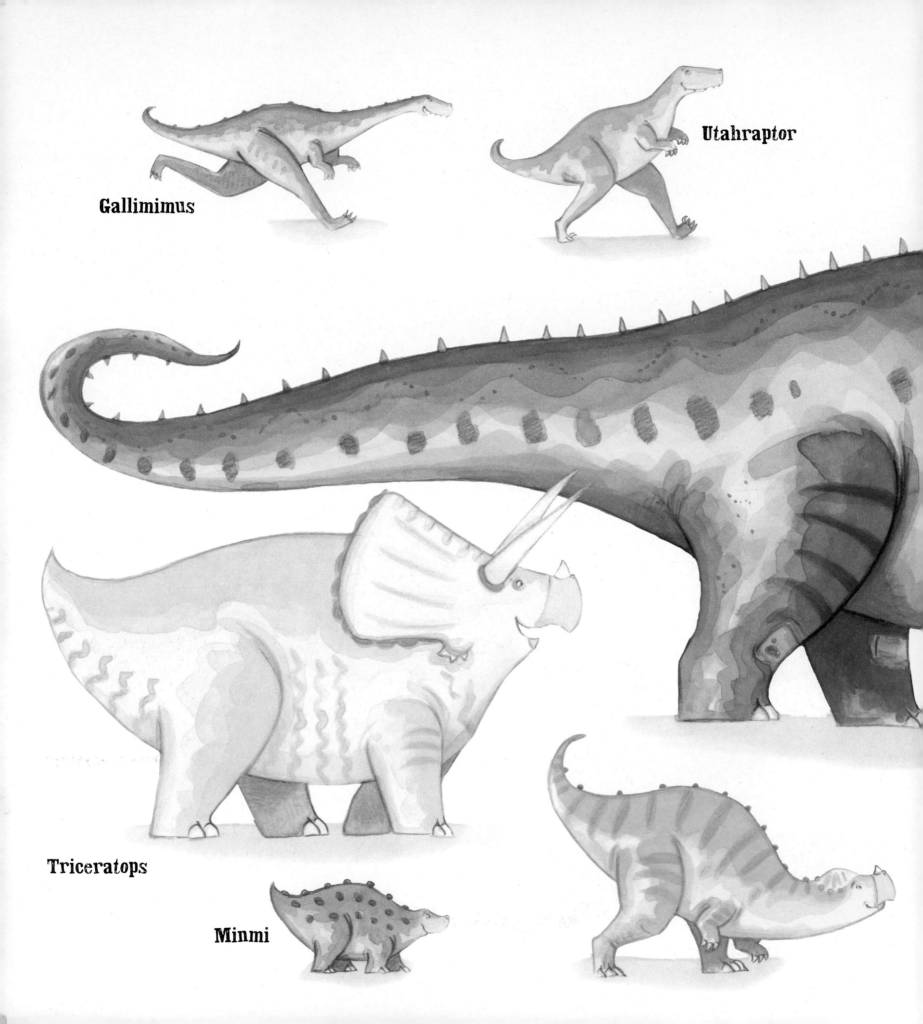

Gallimimus

Utahraptor

Triceratops

Minmi

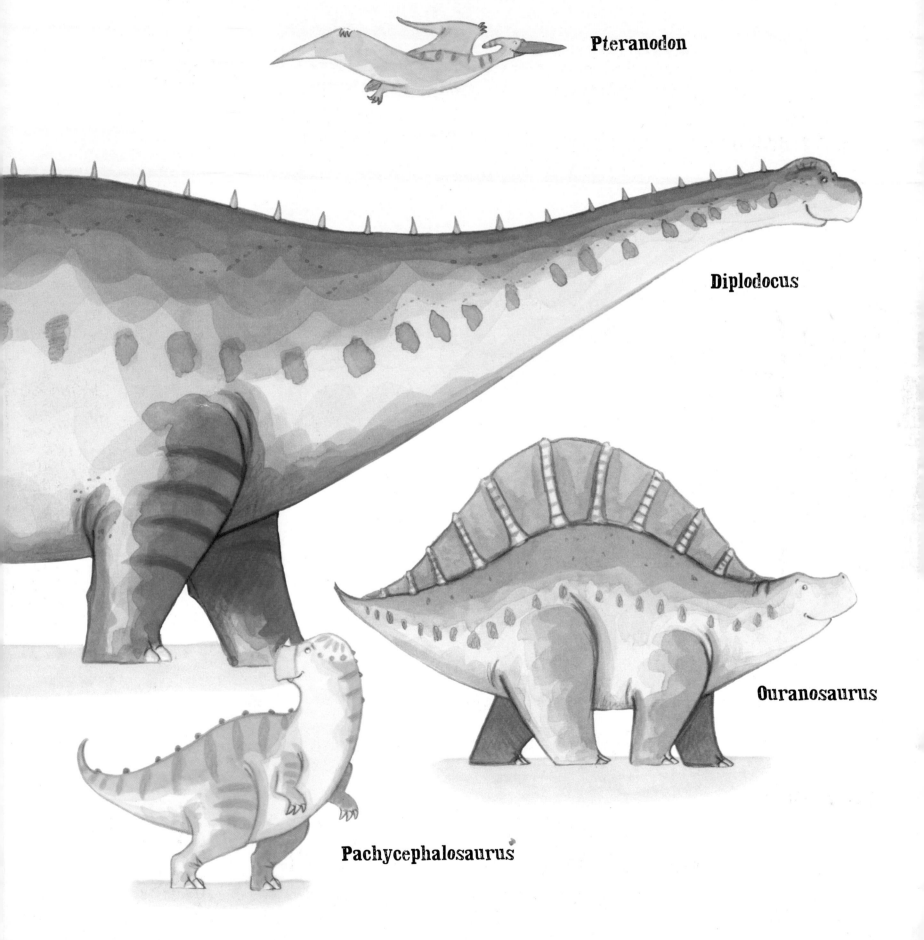

Pteranodon

Diplodocus

Ouranosaurus

Pachycephalosaurus